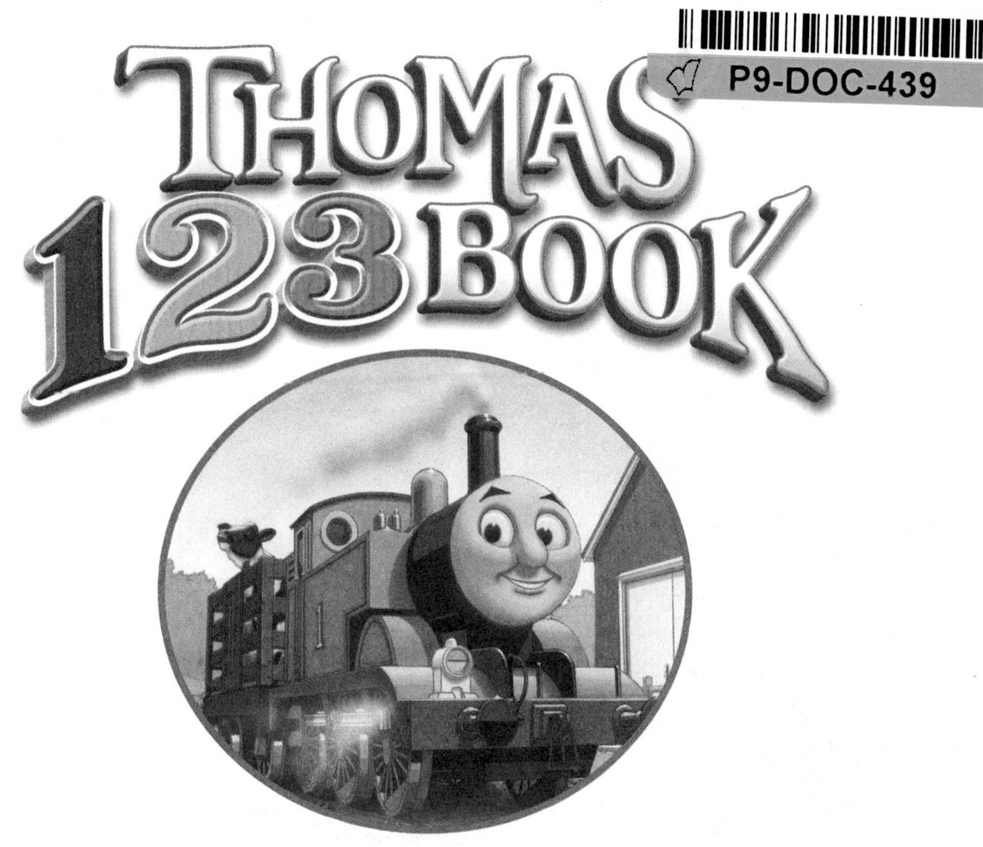

Illustrated by Richard Courtney

A Random House PICTUREBACK® Book

Random House New York

Thomas the Tank Engine & Friends™

CREATED BY BRITT ALLCROFT

Based on The Railway Series by The Reverend W Awdry.

 Published in the United States by Random House Children's Books, a division of Random House, Inc., 1745 Broadway, New York, NY 10019, and in Canada by Random House of Canada Limited, Toronto. Picturebook, Random House, and the Random House colophon are registered trademarks of Random House, Inc.
randomhouse.com/kids
www.thomasandfriends.com
ISBN: 978-0-307-98203-2
Printed in the United States of America
10 9 8 7 6 5 4 3 2
Random House Children's Books supports the First Amendment and celebrates the right to read.

Count along with Thomas and his friends!

Thomas and Edward are chugging to the farm.
Thomas is carrying one cow.

Edward is carrying two bales of hay.
"Moo!" says Edward.

Henry and Gordon count
their cars.
Henry is pulling three cars.

4

Gordon is pulling
four cars.
Which engine has more cars?

James and Percy have important jobs today. James is bringing five milk cans from the farm.

Percy is carrying six mailbags from the post office.
"We're being Really Useful!" peeps Percy.

7

Toby and Emily are helping
Sir Topham Hatt prepare for a sailing race.
Toby brings seven sailboats.

8

Emily drops off eight bright buoys.
"Ahoy, Sir!" peeps Emily.

9

Annie and Clarabel count their passengers.
Annie is carrying nine girls.

Annie

10

Clarabel is carrying ten boys!
The children wave as they pass.

Clarabel

The diesels are working hard at the quarry. Diesel carries eleven wheelbarrows to the quarry.

Mavis is carrying twelve boulders
from the quarry.
"Cheer up, Diesel," says Mavis. "This is fun!"

Harold and Charlie are watching birds.
Harold sees thirteen seagulls.

Charlie sees fourteen ducks.
"Quack, quack!" says Charlie.

Bash and Dash are hauling wood
from Misty Island.
Bash is carrying fifteen boards.

Dash is carrying sixteen logs.
"Come on, Bash. Let's race!" Dash peeps.

Cranky and Salty are working
at the docks.
Cranky is lifting seventeen crates.

Salty is pushing eighteen barrels.
"I wonder what's inside," says Salty.

Kevin and Victor count supplies
at the Steamworks.
Kevin counts nineteen paint cans.

Victor counts twenty spare whistles.
"That's a lot of whistles, boss!" Kevin says.

Let's count again with Thomas!

1

2

3

4

5

6

7

8

9

10

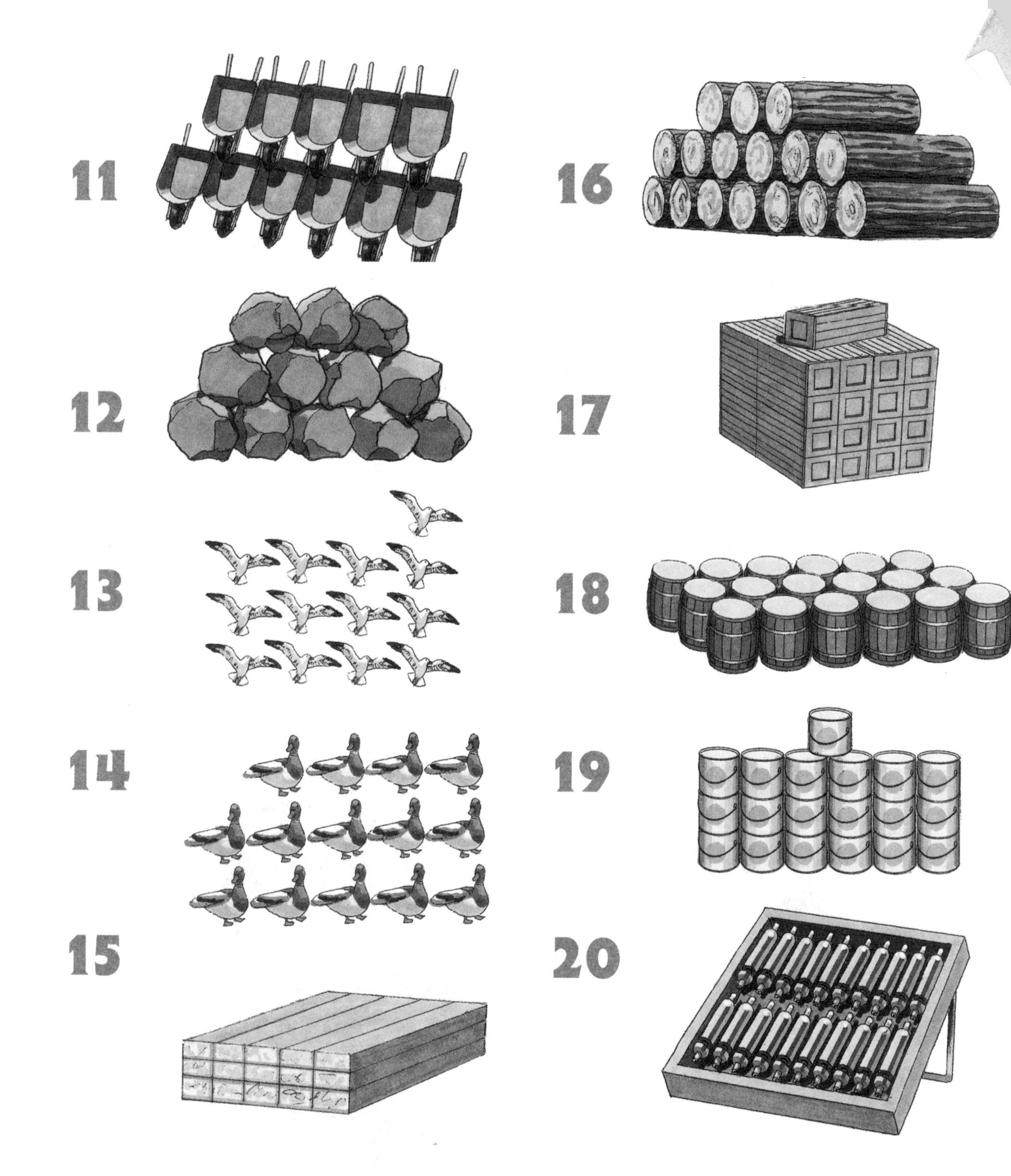
11
12
13
14
15
16
17
18
19
20

It's a busy counting day on the Island of Sodor!